Tim POSSiBLE

& All That Buzz

Also by **AXEL MAISY**

Tim Possible & the
Time-Traveling T. Rex

TiM POSSiBLE
& All That Buzz

· Axel Maisy ·

ALADDIN

New York   London
Toronto   Sydney   New Delhi

ALADDIN

An imprint of Simon & Schuster Children's Publishing Division
1230 Avenue of the Americas, New York, New York 10020
First Aladdin hardcover edition February 2023
Copyright © 2023 by Alexis Bautista Pradas
For information about special discounts for bulk purchases, please contact
Simon & Schuster Special Sales at 1-866-506-1949 or business@simonandschuster.com.
The Simon & Schuster Speakers Bureau can bring authors to your live event.
For more information or to book an event contact the Simon & Schuster Speakers Bureau
at 1-866-248-3049 or visit our website at www.simonspeakers.com.
Cover designed by Karin Paprocki
Interior designed by Mike Rosamilia
The illustrations for this book were rendered digitally.
The text of this book was set in Avenir Next.
Manufactured in the United States of America 1222 FFG
2 4 6 8 10 9 7 5 3 1
Library of Congress Control Number 2022936643
ISBN 9781534492721 (hc)
ISBN 9781534492738 (ebook)

To JACKO, my best friend,
loving wife, head cheerleader,
and mother extraordinaire

TiM POSSiBLE

& All That Buzz

MEET THE HEROES

This is Tim Sullivan. He drank Oskar's IMPOSSIBLE JUICE™, and now all his worries turn into reality.

This is Tito Delgado. He reads comic books and laughs in the face of danger.

This is Oskar. He is a *T. rex*. And an unpredictable time-traveling genius.

THIS STORY

Meet best friends Tim and Tito. Tim is the kid freaking out on the left, with the big eyes and the spiky hair. Tito is the kid freaking out on the right, with the mushroom cut and a half-chewed pickle bite in his mouth. And you might be wondering, Why are they sweating like hairy pigs in

Meet the ten-thousand-pound fly, an unnaturally oversized insect that wraps all the yuckiness of an ordinary fly into a terrifying elephant-sized package.

How did this happen? Will Tim and Tito end up being slurped up by the giant fly? Will they become the world's first fourth-grader-flavored Slurpee? And where's the wacky time-traveling dinosaur this time around?

Those are all fantastic questions, but to answer them, let's restart this story. . . .

PART 1

ONCE UPON A WORRY

CHAPTER 1

THE BEGINNING

··· FRIDAY ···

It was almost noon, and in true Leaping Cobra Elementary School (LCES) fashion, Ms. Hiss had decided to end math class with a **BANG!** So there she was, her fingers racing over the banjo strings while twenty fourth graders sang "Horatio and His Ratio," a catchy yet highly educational song about division.

Not every kid in class was singing, though. Tim was fidgeting, conspicuously silent. Something was troubling him. Was it the time-traveling dinosaur living in his backyard? Was it the fact that ever since he'd mistakenly drunk the IMPOSSIBLE JUICE™, all his worries turned into reality? Or was it perhaps his long-held suspicion that all the nice things that happened in his school were part of some nefarious agenda? It was none of the above. That morning Tim had a much bigger concern.

Oblivious to the frolics around him, Tim checked the wall clock for the hundredth time, and a drop of cold sweat trickled down his back. *Two more minutes till the bell rings,* he thought. *And then . . .* Tim swallowed hard. *I'll talk to her. I HAVE TO!* Tim's gaze darted toward a desk two rows ahead. There a girl laughed, clapped, and sang to the tune, just like everyone else—only much, much better.

Meet Zoe A. Charms, the nicest, coolest, most popular kid at LCES. Zoe was the captain of the volleyball team and a three-time spelling bee champion, and she'd recently been voted LCES's student most likely to win a Nobel Prize. She was kind, she was funny, she was friendly.... She was nothing short of AWESOME, and everyone loved chatting with her!

Well, not everyone. There was one notable exception. A kid who got flustered so much at the mere sight of her that he hadn't been able to utter a single word in front of the girl ever since they'd first met back in kindergarten.

Hi, my name is Zoe. That's a cool eraser! What's your name?

YES, that kid was Tim. And things hadn't gotten easier over time.

She must think I'm an oddball. But that stops TODAY! Tim was determined to talk to Zoe, but his newfound resolve didn't last long. Eighteen seconds, to be exact.

17 . . . 16 . . .

Ms. Hiss ended "Horatio and His Ratio" with an epic banjo solo.

15 . . . 14 . . .

As the last note faded, nineteen kids and a time-traveling dinosaur pretending to be a kid broke out in thunderous applause.

13 . . . 12 . . .

RIIIIING! The bell rang.

11 . . . 10 . . .

Tim stood up and took one step toward Zoe.

Come on, Tim, you can do this!

9 . . . 8 . . .

Zoe turned around, and Tim's heart skipped a beat.

7 . . . 6 . . .

Tim gulped.

Can I, though?

5 . . . 4 . . .

I mean, why would she want to talk to me?

3 . . .

She's so awesome and I'm . . . ME!

2 . . .

Even my superpower is lousy, so . . .

1 . . .

An ominous flutter bubbled in Tim's stomach. *WHAT IF she hates . . . ?*

Tim froze midthought, suddenly aware that one more word would turn his worry into a reality. He panicked. *I can't let that happen. I have to think of something else!* It was a good plan, and at that moment there were millions of nice and perfectly safe things that could've popped into Tim's mind, and that would've been the end of it. But Tim was a worrier. And what do worriers do? They worry impossible worries, which never come true unless . . . Well, unless the worrier is Tim.

Just like that, the impossible turned into unlikely, the unlikely into plausible, the plausible into possible, the possible into likely, and the likely into certain, and out of nowhere, **BAM!** the school was hit by a SALT-STORM, which is kind of like a sandstorm, but way saltier.

CHAPTER 2

WHAT FRIENDS ARE FOR

A few minutes and eighty-three metric tons of salt later, Tim, Tito, and Oskar took seats in the school's cafeteria. Tim shifted uncomfortably. Not only had he failed once again to talk to Zoe, but his worry had left everything (and everyone) covered in a layer of salt.

"I'm so sorry, really," Tim said, all hunched down, his voice barely a whisper. "Ever since I drank the IMPOSSIBLE JUICE™, I feel like a walking disaster."

"Well, there's no need for you to feel like that. Look behind you," said Tito, pointing to the big glass windows that overlooked one of the school's playgrounds.

The space, now blanketed in white, was packed with kids having all sorts of fun.

There were SALT-BALL fights, the ground was pocked with SALT ANGELS, and right by the monkey bars someone had built a huge SALTMAN that bore an uncanny resemblance to Mr. Balboa, the PE teacher.

"See?" said Tito. "Thanks to your power, everyone is having a blast!"

"And that's not all," said Oskar. "Thanks to you, Tito has gained a superpower of his own."

"Seriously?" asked Tito, with a surprised look on his face.

"Sure," said Oskar, grinning. "Let me show you. All you need to do is lean your head, tap it gently like this—**TAP, TAP, TAP**—and **TA-DAAA!**" A drizzle of salt fell from Tito's ear onto the food tray below. "Behold the amazing power of the HUMAN SALTSHAKER!"

The three friends roared with laughter.

"Henceforth I shall be known as the MIGHTY SEASONER," declared Tito. "Excuse me, sir, but your food looks kind of bland," he said, leaning toward Tim. "Here, let me help you."

"NO WAY!" said Tim, blocking his plate with his arms. "That's so disgusting. You're a villain. 'The YUCKY SEASONER' is more like it!"

These antics went on for a while, and by the time the laughter died down, Tim felt as if a heavy burden had been lifted from his shoulders.

"You two are the best, you know," Tim said, still smiling. "I feel much better now. Thank you."

"AH, don't mention it," said Tito, peeling the foil off the top of his daily bocadillo and taking a massive bite. "THATF WHATF FRIENDFS ARE FORF."

Side Note: Some of you might have noticed that Oskar isn't wearing his Misdirection Specs 3.0 anymore. So you might be wondering, How does he manage to blend in with the other students?

CHAPTER 3
PICKLES

The rest of lunch passed uneventfully until, out of nowhere, Zoe appeared next to them, and Tim nearly sprayed his apple juice all over the ceiling.

"Hi. Would you like to try a pickle?" she asked, revealing a tray full of paper cups, each containing a tiny pickled cucumber. "The foodie club is using some of the salt outside to make a new batch, so I'm helping them to share these around. Take one. They're so good!"

Tim froze. In an instant his entire body had become stiffer than a dried cuttlefish!

"Sure, thanks," said Tito, reaching out to take a pickle.

"I'll take one too!" said Oskar. "I've heard of these thingies before, but I never knew they looked so funny. Are they always so tiny and wrinkled?"

"I think these are extra tiny and extra wrinkled," explained Tito, popping the pickle into his mouth. "ANDF EFXTRA YUMMYF!"

Laughing, Zoe turned toward Tim. "Would you like one too?" she asked, with the sweetest smile in sweet-smile history.

Tim's face went through a whole rainbow of colors while his eyes jumped from the tray to Zoe and from Zoe to the tray. Half of Tim's brain was screaming for him to say something. The other half wanted to bury his head under the table like an ostrich. Tim didn't know what to do—both sides of his brain made really good points!

"What's wrong, Tim?" asked Oskar. "Your cheeks are red. Is it because you love pickles too?"

Tim glanced at Oskar with murderous eyes, but then caught a glimpse of Zoe, and he lowered them once again.

"Come on, Tim, you can do it," whispered Tito. "Say something. This is your chance!"

Tito's encouragement was the push that Tim needed. *Okay, I'll do it!* He took a deep breath, opened his mouth, and was about to utter his very first word to Zoe, when a familiar chirpy voice echoed across the room.

CHAPTER 4
THE NEW STUDENT

The singsong voice belonged to Ms. Crawley, the school principal, who stood on the stage by the cafeteria's entrance. Tim frowned. Even though Ms. Crawley was considered by many students to be the nicest human to ever walk the earth, he had a slightly different opinion.

She's the worst!

Tim suspected—NO, HE KNEW—that Ms. Crawley, with all her nice surprise parties and all her nice, sweet words, was WAY TOO NICE to be a real principal. She was hiding something, and over the years, he'd developed several theories regarding her secret.

WHO'S MS. CRAWLEY, REALLY?

(1) Wanted criminal—using LCES to hide from justice?

(2) Evil witch?
- ~~gloves~~
- ~~large nose holes~~
- ~~as bald as a boiled egg~~
- ~~no toes~~
- blue spit—maybe?

(3) Chupacabra in a human costume?

The answer was still a mystery, but one thing was for sure. Whatever Ms. Crawley was, she was evil to the core.

"Gooooooood afternoon, everyone!" said Ms. Crawley, her playful voice booming through the speakers. "How are WE doing on this unusually salty day?"

"GREAAAAAAT!" cried the kids gathered in the cafeteria.

"Well, I'm sure glad to hear it," she said. "But what if I told you that your great day is about to become FUN-tastic? Would you like that?"

"YEEEEEEEES!" roared the crowd.

"Then you're in luck, because I have a wonderful announcement to make."

Everyone hushed.

"As you all know, next Monday we'll be celebrating our annual My Talented Pet Day, where you're all encouraged to bring your pets to school for a day filled with fun and laughter."

Tim sighed. Of all Ms. Crawley's celebrations, My Talented Pet Day was the worst. How was he supposed to enjoy the day when he didn't even have a pet?

Oh my! Theff areff ffo goofff!

Unless . . . Does he count as a pet?

"This year, though, My Talented Pet Day will be EXTRA SPECIAL," continued Ms. Crawley. "And it's all thanks to a bright, generous young man who will be joining Ms. Hiss's fourth-grade class starting today. Would you like to meet him so he can tell you all about it?"

"YEEEEEEEES!" the crowd cheered.

A new fourth grader? Tim perked up.

Ms. Crawley motioned for a tall, blond kid to join her onstage. He was dressed in a perfectly tailored sweat suit, and his smile, wide and pearly white, shone with the unwavering confidence of a movie star. Tim squinted to see him better. The kid's face looked vaguely familiar, but he couldn't quite place it, until . . .

"Please welcome with your cheerfullest cheer the newest member of our loving family:

"WILLIAM WOODROW WIGGLE THE THIRD!"

Tim gasped as a flood of long-forgotten memories washed over him. Tim knew this boy. He was the richest, snootiest, most conceited kid in the Western Hemisphere. He was Tim's true nemesis. The bane of his existence all the way through preschool. W.

CHAPTER 5

HOLD ON!

Before we continue, there's some essential and very important information that you must know regarding William Woodrow Wiggle the Third ("W" for short) and his connection to Tim. You see . . .

It all started years ago when little W and little Tim met in preschool, at the tender age of three. Aw, aren't they adorable?

Little W was the sole heir to one of the biggest fortunes in the world. Little Tim was, well, a normal kid. But despite their different upbringings, the two boys quickly became best friends. And how they laughed! And how they played! It was a wonderful friendship that, sadly, didn't last.

Why, you ask? Because little Tim was way too cheerful, was way too worry-free, and had way too many other friends for little W's liking. YES, Tim was once a popular preschooler. It's hard to believe, right?

Little W was so used to getting everything he wanted, and to being the center of everyone's attention, that he simply couldn't stand being around someone so much happier and so much more popular than him. And so jealousy turned into resentment, and resentment turned into hate, and before long . . . Well, everyone knows that preschoolers can be awfully mean, so you can imagine.

Many things happened during those two years of preschool, and even though it wouldn't be fair to blame little W for turning cheerful little Tim into the anxious worrywart that he is today, W certainly didn't help. It's no wonder, then, that when five-year-old Tim found out that five-year-old W was moving abroad to study in a fancy-schmancy elementary school, Tim breathed with relief.

All those things went through Tim's mind while the crowd cheered W's name. The kid had a ridiculously long name, so the cheering went on for quite a while, which gave Tim plenty of time to consider all his options:

(A) Move to Australia.

(B) Join the army.

(C) Buy a fake mustache and hope that W can't recognize him.

Eventually, in a rare display of self-control and maturity, Tim decided to give W a second chance. *Who knows? He might have changed. Just because he's back, it doesn't mean that my life is about to get harder.*

It doesn't, right?

CHAPTER 6

THE ANNOUNCEMENT

"Thank you, Ms. Crawley. You're too kind," said W, snatching the microphone from the principal's hand. "And thank you all for such a warm welcome. I know that my name is quite a mouthful, so please call me 'W.'"

"Haven't we seen this kid before?" asked Tito.

There was no answer. Tim had lots on his mind, and Oskar was too busy licking the pickle juice from Zoe's tray to pay any attention.

"It's great to be back in Metrosalis after so many years abroad," continued W. "Some of you might not know, but it was my great-great-great-great-great-grandfather, the legendary Wild Wyatt Wiggle, who founded this town back in 1848."

There were a few **GASPs** of surprise in the audience, and Tim rolled his eyes.

"Since then, the Wiggle family has called this wonderful place home, and Wiggle Industries, the leading supplier of live worms and other live fishing bait, remains the largest employer in town."

"He must be loaded," whispered Tito. "Like madre-mía-super-mega rich!"

Tim rolled his eyes some more.

"As for myself, some of you might remember me from last Friday, when I cut short my school visit to face a deranged robot that was attacking this cafeteria."

Wait, WHAT? thought Tim, startled.

"That's right!" said Tito. "I knew his face looked familiar. I saw him during SARA's attack!"

"I risked my life to save you all, that's true," continued W. "But PLEASE don't call me a hero."

OF COURSE WE SHOULDN'T CALL YOU A HERO! You didn't defeat the robot. WE DID! That's what Tim wanted to scream, but he didn't. He and Tito had agreed not to mention the incident, to avoid calling too much attention to Oskar.

"Anyway, enough about me. I hate talking about myself. Hoo, hoo, hoo!" W cackled.

At this, Tim would have rolled his eyes even more, but his pupils were already halfway down his back.

"So let's talk about the surprise I've prepared for My Talented Pet Day instead. You see, when Ms. Crawley told me how much you all looked forward to bringing your pets to school next Monday, I thought: *Why don't we organize a proper talent show? Wouldn't that be fun?* So I pulled some strings, made a few calls, and I'm happy to announce that next Monday you're all invited to the very first My Most Talented Pet Competition! And let me tell you, it will be AWESOME. We'll have famous guest judges, it will be broadcast live on YouCube, and best of all, the student with the most talented pet will receive the coolest prize in the history of pet competitions."

There was a brief moment of startled silence, followed by thunderous applause.

W waved left and right, a smug smile on his face. When the cheering died down, Ms. Crawley thanked the kid again, and the announcement concluded with everyone chanting the school song about cobras leaping into the future.

"Next Monday is going to be GREAT!" said Tito. "There isn't a pet more talented than Dr. Curtis, so that prize is as good as mine."

"I wouldn't be so sure," teased Zoe. "Wait till you see what my Waffles can do."

Everyone was excited, and despite his silence, Tim had to admit that it was surprisingly generous of W to organize all that for his new schoolmates. *Perhaps having him around won't be so bad after all,* he thought. *All I have to do is avoid him, and with any luck, he might not even remember me.*

But no sooner had Tim finished his thought than W walked toward him. "OH, there you are. I thought that was you!"

CHAPTER 7

HERE COMES TROUBLE

Tim, certain that he'd been recognized, considered once again his options:

(A) Put on a fake smile and greet W like a long-lost friend.

(B) Run away and never look back.

Hey! Isn't that a blue-whale mariachi?

(C) Use his power to worry a distraction.

But before Tim could make a decision, W zipped past him, as if he didn't exist. *Then who . . . ?* Tim turned around and felt the air leave his lungs. W was on one knee right in front of Zoe!

"It's you, isn't it? The famous Zoe Charms from Instaglam?" he asked.

"Um, yes?" said Zoe, taking a step back.

"OH MY! You look even lovelier in real life!" W extended a hand toward Zoe. "I'm at your service, my lady."

WHAT? Tim stared at the scene with burning eyes, and he was about to give that arrogant slimeball a piece of his mind, when Zoe took care of things.

"Thank you for offering to help. Please take this," she said, surprising W by placing an empty tray on his hand. "It looks like we've run out of pickles. Would you be so kind as to go to the foodie club upstairs and tell them that we need some more?"

"Yes, we do!" cheered Oskar.

W startled. "Sh-sh-sure, but . . ."

"Oh, and please don't kneel on the ground," Zoe added. "You might ruin your clothes with all the pickle juice on the floor."

AHHH! The rich kid shrieked, leaping to his feet so fast that he almost dropped the tray all over himself. While W checked and rechecked his clothes for any stains, Tim tried hard not to burst out in laughter.

"By the way, I have a question," said Tito. "Can you tell us what that supercool prize next Monday is going to be?"

"I hope it's a truckload of pickles!" said Oskar.

W tsk-tsked. "You'll find out on Monday. It's a secret," he said, not even bothering to look in their direction.

"Oh, that's too bad," said Zoe. "I'm very curious too."

In an instant, W was back to his slimy self. "Well, that changes things. I can't say no to such a lovely lady, can I?" Then he placed the tray on the table and reached into his sweatshirt pocket. "Here, let me show you."

Tim and Tito looked at each other, and this time they both rolled their eyes.

W pulled something out very slowly. It was a . . .
Pack of PopPop Pearls?

"I know what you're thinking," said W with a grin. "But no, this is NOT a regular pack of PopPop Pearl candy. You see, I love PopPop Pearls, but I've always wished that they had a much poppier pop. Last month I called the owners of the company and suggested that they give it a try, but to my surprise, they refused. They thought that it was too dangerous, and way too expensive. So what did I do? I bought the company. Four weeks and three hundred and fifty million dollars later, here it is, a one-of-a-kind treasure: a pack of the poppiest PopPop Pearls in history!"

"WOOOOOOOW!" said Tito, rubbing his hands while he salivated in front of the pack of candy. "I can't wait to try them after I win next Monday."

W snickered. "That's funny. You think you can win?"

"Why not?" asked Tito, frowning. "My pet iguana is extremely talented, you know?"

"That might be the case," said W. "But I'll be

joining the competition too, and let me assure you, my pet's talent is second to none. HOO, HOO, HOO!"

Wait. Is W joining the competition too? Now everything made sense! "This whole thing is a ruse to show off your fancy pet!" blurted Tim.

Tim covered his mouth. He hadn't meant to say that aloud, and he regretted it at once; but it was too late. Tito, Oskar, W, and Zoe were all staring right at him.

CHAPTER 8

THE BET

"EXCUSE ME?" asked W, sizing Tim up.

"I . . . So . . . I . . ." Tim hesitated, uncomfortably aware that Zoe was looking at him.

"Wait a minute, waaaaaait a minute," said W, narrowing his eyes and sending a chill down Tim's spine. "That spiky hair. I know you. YOU'RE TIM!"

W hooted with laughter, and Tim's face lost what little color it'd had left.

"So you two already knew each other?" asked Oskar.

Tim shrugged. With Zoe around, he wouldn't be able to explain.

"Oh yes, Tim and I go a loooong way back," said W, winking. "Right, Shimmy Timmy?"

Tim's face reddened. It was preschool all over again!

"You shouldn't call people names," said Zoe. "That's not nice."

"Oh, don't worry," said W. "He used to love that nickname."

NO, I DIDN'T! I HATED IT! thought Tim.

"Anyway, tell me, Tim, will you bring your pet to perform next Monday too?" the snooty kid asked.

Tim lowered his eyes and shrank a little.

"That's what I thought. There's no way some-one like you can train a pet. I bet you don't even have one!" W said, and laughed.

"OF COURSE HE DOES!" yelled Tito, placing his arm over Tim's shoulder.

I DO? thought Tim, confused.

W raised an eyebrow. "Does he?" he asked, sounding doubtful.

"OH YES! And it's the coolest, most talented pet ever," added Tito. "I would be worried if I were you. Tim's definitely going to win those PopPop Pearls that you love so much."

Tim knew that Tito was trying to defend him, but he didn't like where things were going.

"Well, if he's so sure, then why don't we make a bet?" asked W. "What do you say, Tim? Are you in?"

Tim looked from W to Tito and from Tito to W. "B-b-but," he stuttered.

"OH, HE'S TOTALLY IN, SO VERY IN!" declared Tito, shaking Tim's body as he spoke.

Tim tried to catch Tito's eyes. *WHAT ARE YOU DOING?*

"So here's the bet," said W, looking at Tim. "If I win, you'll have to come to school dressed as Poppy McPoppins—PopPop Pearl's popular purple mascot—for ONE WHOLE WEEK. And don't worry about the costume. I'll get it for you."

Judging from W's smile, Tim was sure that it wouldn't be a flattering outfit.

"DONE!" said Tito. "But if Tim wins—"

"You'll get him a truckload of pickles!" added Oskar. "Tim loooooves pickles."

WHAAAT? But before Tim could say anything, his friends were already shaking W's hand and the deal was done.

Tim stood motionless, almost in shock. All around him the crowd of students started to head back to their classrooms, and, claiming that he had some urgent business to take care of, W left too.

Why do these things keep happening to me? Tim wondered. *What am I gonna do?* Tim was lost in his own thoughts when he heard someone talking to him. "I didn't know you also had a pet. Well, I hope you win. I'll be cheering for you!"

"Thank you," he said, almost without thinking. But then, *Wait a minute, didn't that voice sound familiar?* Tim looked up and saw Zoe smiling and waving goodbye.

In an instant, W, the pet competition, the bet, they all disappeared from his mind. He smiled and waved back awkwardly. "I did it," he mumbled.

"YES, YOU DID!" said Tito, patting Tim's back. "You talked to Zoe, and look, there's no SALT-STORM in sight!"

CHAPTER 9
TWO CHANCES

Tim's momentary happiness didn't last, and on his way back home with Tito and Oskar, he kind of lost it.

"WHAT WERE YOU THINKING?" he yelled, almost in tears. "You know that there's NO WAY I can beat W. I don't even have a pet!

"Next Monday I'm going to look like a fool," he continued. "And then, when that conceited monster and his super-fancy pet end up winning, I'll have to wear a ridiculous costume for a whole week. A WHOLE WEEK! I'll be the laughingstock of the entire school," he said, and groaned.

Things were not looking up for poor Tim, but on the bright side, he was so sure of the impending disaster that he didn't make it certain by worrying about it. Because of that, he still had a chance. Well, two chances, actually.

"Relaaaax," said Oskar. "Have you forgotten that you're friends with a very ingenious, funny, and may I add good-looking time-traveling dinosaur? I can build you the coolest pet you've ever seen!"

That was chance number one. And in the time that it took the three friends to reach Tim's backyard, Oskar listed three hundred seventy-five possible pets he could create.

What about a saber-toothed tiger that
drinks lava and spits fire?

Or a giant rhinoceros
that poops fancy
designer furniture?

How about a
big-eared elephant
that can fly?

I know! A chicken that
can lay chocolate eggs.
And race monster trucks!

But even though Tim considered Oskar's offer for a second, at the end he decided to pass.

After what happened with SARA, I think it's safer if you don't get involved this time.

AW, MAN!

Clearly disappointed, Oskar disappeared into his lair. Which brings us to chance number two.

"My plan is simple," said Tito. "We know that you can turn your worries into reality, right?"

"Yes." Tim nodded. "So?"

Tito smiled. "Elementary, my dear friend. All you need to do to get your own super-talented pet IS TO WORRY ABOUT IT!"

Tim raised an eyebrow. "Right. And how do you suggest that I do that? I can't even control my normal worries!"

"Not yet, but you're getting really close," insisted Tito. "The SALT-STORM wasn't half-bad, and there's no one better at worrying than you, that's for sure! Come on, Tim, I believe in you!"

Tim sighed. The truth of the matter was that he had no other options, and if Tito was right and his plan worked . . . Tim smiled, picturing W's defeat. "Okay, let's do it. Let's give it a try!"

CHAPTER 10

HOW (NOT) TO WORRY YOUR PET

Following Tito's instructions, Tim closed his eyes and tried to picture a pet. "I'll try to worry a dog," he said, smiling. Tim loved dogs, and he'd always wanted one.

But an ordinary pet wouldn't be enough to win, so Tim tried to imagine that his dog could do all sorts of amazing tricks.

Like playing chess like a pro,

speaking perfect Chinese,

sniffing out hidden treasure,

and riding the flying trapeze!

The tricky part came next.

"Now you have to turn what you've imagined into a worry," explained Tito.

But that was easier said than done. Tim cleared his throat, and with the image of his perfect dog fixed in his mind, he said:

"OH NO! WHAT IF I had that perfect dog? Wouldn't that be awful?"

Tim reopened his eyes and waited with bated breath for his worry to work its magic and his amazing pet to appear. He waited, and waited, and waited, and when nothing happened, all his hope and excitement crumbled like a house of cards. Tim sighed. "I can't do it."

"Don't say that. I know you can!" said Tito. "I think the problem is that you were just PRE-TENDING to be worried."

A wave of anger surged through Tim. "OF COURSE I WAS PRETENDING TO BE WORRIED!" he yelled. "How do you expect me to *really* worry about something that I want? That's impossible!"

Tito shook his head. "You should know by now that 'impossible' doesn't apply to you anymore, my friend. Trust me. If anyone can figure this out, it's you."

Deep inside, Tim knew that Tito was trying to help, but he'd had a terrible day and his frustration boiled over.

"But what if you're wrong?" he snapped. "I might have a superpower, but look at me. I'm no superhero!" A pang of self-doubt fluttered in Tim's stomach, but he ignored it. "I'm lousy, my power is lousy. So WHAT IF the only pet I can worry about is the lousiest pet of all?"

Tim stopped. He knew what he had done, but there was nothing he could do about it. The impossible turned into unlikely, the unlikely into plausible, the plausible into possible, yada, yada, yada, until, out of nowhere, **POOF!** Something appeared right in front of them.

There it was. Tim's only hope of defeating W.
His first pet ever: a fly.

At that point things were looking so bleak
that you might have expected Tim to spiral into a
full-blown meltdown, creating a worry so impos-
sibly dangerous that it would blow up the planet
and destroy reality as we know it. However, that's
not what happened. Because once the reality of
being a pet owner started to sink in, Tim started
to feel much, much better.

"You know what? A fly is not so bad," said Tim, petting the insect's back with a finger. "It's an original pet!"

Tito nodded. "Yeah, and imagine how cool it would be if we could teach it some tricks. You might even have a shot to win!"

That was a fantastic idea. "We should totally do that," Tim decided. "But first," he said, turning his attention back to the fly, "let's give you a name."

CHAPTER 11
MARGOT

··· SUNDAY ···

Meet Margot, Tim's pet. And in case you're wondering, YES, she's still a common housefly. And in case you're wondering, NO, there's still nothing special about her—all she does is buzz around and slurp up grains of sugar. What did you expect? She's a COMMON housefly, after all!

It was Sunday morning, and Tim and Tito had spent the last day and a half trying to train Margot to do tricks. To say that they were finding it challenging would be a massive understatement. No matter how many times they explained, or how many sweet treats they offered her, Margot would ignore them and do her thing.

"I'm sorry, Tim, but this is useless," said Tito, throwing his hands into the air. "We've used a whole bag of sugar, and she hasn't learned a thing yet. I think it's time to face the facts: Margot is dumb."

"Don't say that!" said Tim, covering Margot (and her tiny fly ears) so she wouldn't hear the terrible thing that Tito had said. "Don't mess with her confidence. She's starting to get it now. Look. Margot, SIT!"

Margot flew all the way to Tim's cheek, and Tito broke into laughter.

"You're right, Tim, she's almost there," he teased, tears rolling down his face.

"Okay, okay, you have a point," sighed Tim. "Margot, I hope you don't take this the wrong way, but you're kind of clueless." Margot tickled Tim's cheek with her tiny legs, and Tim laughed. "But I like you anyway."

"So what are you gonna do about tomorrow?" asked Tito. "There's not much time left."

Tim let out a long, slow exhale. "Yeah, it's not looking good. Perhaps it's time to change schools, or countries if possible."

"Well, before you consider that," said Tito, "there's still another chance." He pointed toward the old boat standing in Tim's backyard, where Oskar had built his amazing secret lair.

Tim thought about all the things that could go wrong if he used one of Oskar's inventions, but then he thought about all the things that would CERTAINLY go wrong if he didn't, and that made up his mind.

"Okay, let's see if we can find him. I hope he's not mad anymore."

CHAPTER 12
HELP

Oskar's lair contained hundreds of levels and thousands of rooms, but Tim and Tito didn't have to spend any time looking for their friend. They found him sitting in the lobby, almost as if he'd been expecting their visit.

"Oh, what a surprise," he said, a wide grin spreading across his green face. "Have you already finished training your new pet?"

"No, we're having a bit of trouble," said Tim, avoiding the dinosaur's eyes. "We came to see if perhaps"—he paused—"you could help?"

Oskar narrowed his eyes. "Huh, I see, but are you sure that you want my help?" he asked. "I thought you didn't want me to get involved because my creations were too 'unpredictable' for you."

Tim shifted his weight from foot to foot. "I . . . I'm sorry I said that," he said finally. "I really need your help. Pleeeeeeease?"

Oskar broke into laughter. "Relax, I'm teasing you," he said. "Of course I'll help. In fact, it's already done! The moment I saw you two playing with your dumb new friend, I knew you'd end up needing it."

"YOU DID?" asked Tim and Tito at once.

"Yes, it's all there," said Oskar, pointing to a glass box that was filled with dirt. "Look."

Tim and Tito approached the box and started to inspect it.

"This looks like Dr. Curtis's terrarium," Tito said, prodding the glass.

"I'm sorry, but I don't get it," said Tim, puzzled. "How is this going to help Margot perform any tricks?"

Oskar handed each of them a magnifying glass. "Perhaps this will help. Now take a closer look."

Tim placed the device over his eye and inspected the soil like a true detective. He first noticed a tunnel, followed by another one, followed by many more. Then he noticed a long line of ants carrying food toward a large space, where an ant with a massive belly—probably the queen—rested quietly.

"What's so special about this?" asked Tim. "It's an ant colony feeding their queen."

"Are you sure that's who they're feeding?" asked Oskar.

Tim looked again and noticed something odd. Oskar was right: the ants were not giving any food to the queen. So who was it for? Tim looked even closer, and then he saw it, right on top of the queen, munching on snacks while sitting on a red ant-sized sofa.

WHO IN THE WORLD IS THAT?

CHAPTER 13
STEVE

Meet Steve, Oskar's test subject for his latest invention, the Bug Brain Booster 3.0.

Steve is an ant, and not a particularly impressive one. He used to be the colony's 137th Chief Handkerchief Carrier, which is a fancy name to say that he spent his days covered in royal snot.

With such a disgusting job, it's not a surprise that Steve had spent his entire short ant life being pushed around by others.

"But look at him now. He's even bossing the queen around!" said Oskar. "And do you want to know how? Here, look. I prepared a promotional leaflet for you two."

ALL NEW!

B.B.B. 3.0
BUG BRAIN BOOSTER

Have you ever dreamed of being the queen bee? *Would you like to have your own personal army of slithering earthworms? Do you wish that you could boss mosquitoes around and tell them all to buzz off? Well, dream no more!*

The Bug Brain Booster 3.0 is the world's first neural enhancer designed to boost and control the minds of creepy-crawlies. Simply put it on like a normal hat, and all the bugs around you will understand and follow your every command.

ORDER NOW!
Call (012) 555-0199
Limited Stock

Five power levels!
Hands-free operation!
Long-lasting battery!

"Pretty neat, right?" said Oskar, removing the hat from Steve's head and handing it to Tim. "It's on the lowest setting now, but that should be plenty to control your fly."

"¡Increíble!" said Tito, inspecting the device in Tim's hand.

"Yeah, sounds great. But how am I supposed to fit this on my head?" asked Tim, holding the tiny hat with two fingers.

"Oh, I almost forgot," said Oskar, grabbing a laser shooter from a table. "All we need to do is shrink that big spiky head of yours, and the hat will fit perfectly. Could you please stay still?"

"WHAAAT? NO WAY! DON'T SHOOT!" yelled Tim.

Oskar's laughter echoed through the lair. "Oh, Tim, you're the funniest. I'm kidding!" he said. "This is my Molecular Ginormizer 5.0, and it makes things grow bigger, not smaller. See?" Oskar aimed the laser at the tiny hat, and **PLOP!** it grew instantly.

Tim sighed in relief.

"Come on, come on, let's go try it out with Margot!" urged Tito.

And that's how two kids, a time-traveling dinosaur, and a fly spent the rest of that Sunday getting ready for Monday's competition. As for poor Steve, well, you can't make everyone happy all the time.

PART 2

YOU WIN SOME, YOU FEAR SOME

CHAPTER 14

My Most Talented Pet Competition

··· MONDAY ···

Monday had finally arrived, and so far My Talented Pet Day had been a huge success. The school was filled with more pets than ever, and it looked like everyone had spent the weekend training hard for the day's main attraction, the My Most Talented Pet Competition.

To host the event, the gym had been transformed into a television studio. Tim looked around, dazzled. It was clear that no expense had been spared. There were cannons—fog cannons, confetti cannons, flame cannons, bubble cannons, and snow cannons. There were cameras—cameras on the ceiling, cameras on the floor, cameras on cranes, cameras on rails, and cameras flying on drones. And there were lights—strobe lights, striplights, spotlights, floodlights, and laser lights. There were so many lights that the entire stage seemed to glow.

WAA!

When the show was about to start, Tim, Tito, and their pets joined the other contestants waiting for their turn behind the stage. There they took seats right by a little screen showing the broadcast. *I wonder if Oskar has managed to get a good spot,* thought Tim as the camera panned through the audience. His thoughts were interrupted by a blast of music bursting from the speakers. The audience broke into cheer.

"It's the judges!" whispered Tito, pointing at the screen. "They're here!"

W hadn't been exaggerating when he'd said that he'd invited famous guest judges. These were the most famous judges of them all. They were:

Simon Catwell—the king of judges. There cannot be a talent show without him. Simon has seen it all and never sugarcoats his opinions.

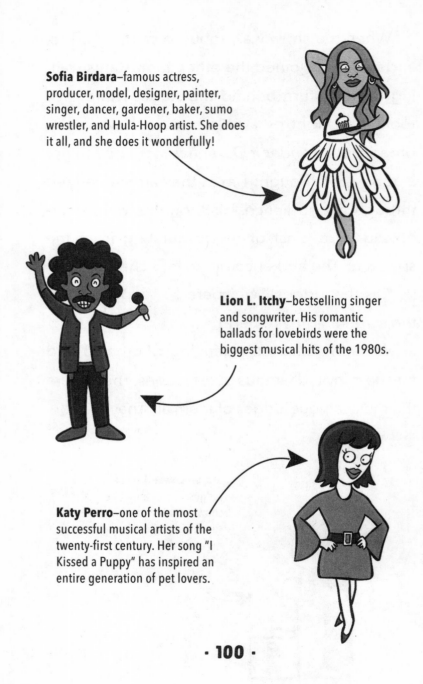

Sofia Birdara–famous actress, producer, model, designer, painter, singer, dancer, gardener, baker, sumo wrestler, and Hula-Hoop artist. She does it all, and she does it wonderfully!

Lion L. Itchy–bestselling singer and songwriter. His romantic ballads for lovebirds were the biggest musical hits of the 1980s.

Katy Perro–one of the most successful musical artists of the twenty-first century. Her song "I Kissed a Puppy" has inspired an entire generation of pet lovers.

Once the judges had been properly intro-
duced, the show started, and an endless parade
of kids with their talented furry and furless
friends performed on the big stage. Tim tried to
keep his mind busy, but it was hard not to stare
at the screen every now and then. Some of the
best acts included a third grader with a small
Chihuahua who could spin taco shells on its tail,
a second grader with a boa who could shape
itself as any short word, and a first grader whose
smart kitten could add and subtract meows.

Tito and Dr. Curtis performed an iguana ball-catching demonstration that also got high praise from the judges. And of course Zoe and her adorable pug, Waffles, did well too. They wowed everyone with a gracefully synchronized dance routine. But unsurprisingly, it was W and his fancy-schmancy pet who stole the show.

His one-of-a-kind crocotoodle, a bird who had long been considered extinct, performed a crocotoodling concert worthy of a major record label deal. They were good, ridiculously good, and it seemed inevitable that they would be crowned the winners. But there was one more act left. Tim took a little plastic box from his pocket and adjusted the strange hat on his head. *Let's go, Margot. It's showtime!*

CHAPTER 15
A STAR IS BORN

Tim swallowed hard and stepped onto the stage, his heart pounding. He knew that everyone was looking at him, but thankfully the lights were so bright that he couldn't see beyond the judges' table.

"Please tell us your name," said Ms. Birdara.

"My name . . . uh . . . My name's Tim."

"Hello, Tim, nice to meet you," said Mr. Catwell. "You're our last contestant, but I'm a bit puzzled. Where's your pet?"

"Oh yes, yes," said Tim, fumbling with the plastic box he was carrying. Finally it opened, and he placed Margot on his hand. "Here it is. Her name is Margot. She's my . . . pet fly."

There was a second of silence.

"Sorry, did you say 'pet fly'?" asked Ms. Perro.

Tim nodded and tried to ignore the whispers and mocking laughs coming from the audience.

"I gotta tell you, that's a first," added Ms. Perro. "But why not?"

"I can't wait," said Mr. Itchy. "Come on, Tim, show us what you've got!"

Tim wiped a drop of sweat from his brow. It was hot, really hot up there. The lights, the heat, the judges, the audience, any of those would have been an excuse good enough for old Tim to start worrying. But Margot and he had trained way too hard for him to ruin it all, so he took a deep breath and started sending his thoughts to the fly. *Let's do this, Margot, just as we practiced.*

What followed can only be described as the greatest show ever put on by a kid and his pet. There were thrilling stunts, comedy, music, tap dancing, acrobatics, and magic tricks. It was unbelievable! Neither the audience nor the judges could take their eyes from Tim and his fly. They laughed, they cheered, they whistled, they oohed, they aahed, and when the performance finished, they gave Tim and Margot the first and only standing ovation of the day.

"YES!" shouted Mr. Catwell, bouncing on the judges' table. "That's what I'm talking about—pure, raw, original entertainment!"

Tim forced a smile. Mr. Catwell was pretty scary even when he was being nice.

"Unbelievable," continued Mr. Catwell. "I had zero expectations. But, Tim, you've blown my mind. Bravo!" He clapped.

"For once I agree with Simon," said Ms. Birdara. "You came onstage looking like an ordinary kid with an ordinary fly, and you've shown the entire world that you two are nothing short of extraordinary!"

"I couldn't agree more," added Ms. Perro. "That performance was out of this world, and you and your amazing pet are both stars!"

Tim felt his face flush.

"Well, I think it's unanimous, right?" said Mr. Itchy, looking at his fellow judges. They all nodded. "Ladies and gentlemen . . ."

CHAPTER 16

THE PRICE OF FAME

The crowd cheered, the lights flashed, the music boomed, and tons upon tons of sparkly confetti rained down onto Tim. He stood motion-less while happiness, relief, disbelief, and a fair bit of shame fought a battle in his head. He had won, but it was all thanks to Oskar's invention, and even though the rules didn't say that you couldn't use a super-advanced controlling hat to make your pet do amazing feats, he still felt a bit like a cheat.

"Alegra esa cara, you DID IT!" screamed Tito, bringing Tim back to reality by squeezing him with one of his bear hugs.

"TIM! TIM! TIM!" the spectators chanted. Tim stretched his neck over Tito's shoulder and saw that Zoe was at the front of the crowd. When she caught Tim's eye, she smiled and gave him a big thumbs-up. Tim's gaze fell toward the box he was holding while a smile spread across his face. "We've done it, Margot. It worked!"

Then, out of the corner of his eye, Tim noticed W. Jaw clenched and face twisted and red, he was pushing his way toward the judges' table, but his path was blocked. Unable to get any closer, he started yelling and swinging his crocotoodle in the air. But whatever it was that W was trying to achieve, it didn't work. Everyone's attention was on Tim.

The music died down and W, looking much calmer than before, appeared onstage. "And now it's time to present the winner with his well-deserved prize," he announced, practically spitting the words. W turned to face Tim and extended the pack of the poppiest PopPop Pearls in history to him. "Congratulations," he muttered through gritted teeth.

Tim flinched and eyed W's hand as if it were a rattlesnake about to strike. He had dreamed of this moment many times over the weekend, but suddenly he almost regretted winning.

W has always been a sore loser. Is he going to get back at me for this? With one look at his nemesis's icy stare, Tim knew that THAT was exactly what was going through W's mind. *He wants revenge,* Tim realized. *But I don't want any more trouble!*

"Thanks, W, but I don't need any prize," Tim said, motioning for W to keep the candy. "I know how much this pack of PopPop Pearls means to you, so I'd prefer for you to keep it. You and your pet were amazing too!"

"Take the prize," W muttered slowly, his gaze piercing Tim like a dagger. "Don't you dare take pity on me."

Tim gulped and took the candy. W turned back around and thanked everyone for coming, and as soon as he declared the end of the show and the cameras stopped rolling, he darted toward the exit.

But the angry kid had barely taken two steps when Oskar stopped him. "It was a pleasure betting with you, my friend. Here's the address for the delivery," he said, handing W a piece of paper with scribbling on it. "You may leave the truckload of pickles by the old boat in the backyard. We'll take it from there."

W grunted, snatched the piece of paper, and stomped his way backstage.

Tim was about to leave too when Zoe approached him. "That was incredible, Tim. You and Margot deserved that win. I'm so happy for you!"

"Uh, th-thank you, Zo-Zo-Zoe," stuttered Tim, feeling the tips of his ears grow hot. Why was it so hard to talk to her? Zoe smiled and started walking away with Waffles, her pug, in her arms.

Tim racked his brain to think of something else to say. "W-w-wait! I . . . I love . . . pugs. I love pugs too!" he said. But Zoe was already gone.

Would you say you love pugs as much as you love pickles, though?

CHAPTER 17

FAREWELL

Later that day Tim and Tito were sitting
on Tim's bed. In a few hours the video of Margot's
performance had gone viral, and the Sullivans'
phone hadn't stopped ringing since. Everyone
wanted to talk to Tim. He'd even been invited to
appear on *The Early Show with Estevan Cortez*,
the biggest morning show on TV!

"You have to get an autograph from Mr. Cortez. Mi abuelita loves him!" said Tito.

Tim was staring at the plastic box on his lap, deep in thought. *This is what I've always wanted, but . . .* Margot's big innocent eyes pierced right through him, and Tim flushed, feeling a pang of guilt. "I'm sorry, I can't do it. I'm turning it down," he said.

"WHAT? WHY?" asked Tito.

"Because everyone expects Margot to perform again, and I don't like controlling her mind. It feels wrong. It *is* wrong!" he explained.

Tito chuckled. "She's a fly! She would've been crushed or eaten by now if it weren't for you. I bet being mind-controlled is the best thing that could've happened to her."

"But we don't know that, do we?" objected Tim. "Maybe she hates it. Maybe it hurts her somehow. It can't be pleasant to have someone controlling you. I wanted to have a pet, but I've turned her into a puppet instead!"

"Vaya, I hadn't considered that," said Tito. "So, what are you going to do?"

Tim stood up and opened the window.

I'm going to set her free!

Tim unlocked the plastic container and left it on the windowsill. "Goodbye, Margot. You've been a great pet; I'll miss you so much!"

The fly didn't move, though.

"See? She doesn't want to leave," said Tito.

"Of course she does!" insisted Tim. "She's a bit confused, that's all. After so much mind control, I bet she doesn't even remember what she wants." Tim took the Bug Brain Booster 3.0 from his backpack and placed it on his spiky head.

"I'm doing this for you, Margot," he said. *Just one last time.* "I order you to leave this box."

Margot took flight and buzzed around Tim.

"But don't stay here. Fly away! Do your fly thing, be the fly you always wanted to be!"

Margot obeyed. "Thank you," Tim yelled as the fly buzzed deeper into the backyard. "And no matter what, from now on don't ever let anyone tell you what to do!"

And so Tim watched his first and only pet disappear over the bushes. *Farewell, Margot. I'll never forget you,* he thought as he wiped the tears pricking his eyes.

"WOW, that was intense. Who knew that fare-wells could be so hard?" said Oskar, startling Tim, who hadn't heard the dinosaur enter the room. "You know what you need? A pickle!" Oskar dug his hand into a glass jar and popped a pickled cucumber into his mouth. "THEEFF ARF FOOOO AWFEFOME!" he mumbled, munching happily.

"Really? Let me try," said Tito, taking one also. "WOW! ¡Delicioso! Where did you get them?"

"W left a truckload by the boat five minutes ago," explained Oskar. "He was looking for you, Tim, so I told him you were here."

Tim shuddered. He didn't like the idea of W paying him a visit, and his stomach clenched just at the thought of W finding out the truth about how he'd won the competition. Tim shook his head and stopped his worry in time, though. Unfortunately, that didn't make any difference, because W was already there, hidden among the bushes. He'd seen and heard everything about the mind control, and he was seething with the need for revenge.

CHAPTER 18
SURPRISE, SURPRISE

··· TUESDAY ···

Tim woke up with mixed feelings about the day ahead. On the one hand, things were looking up. He was kind of a school celebrity now, and he was finally getting close to Zoe. On the other hand, though, the sting of Margot's departure was still fresh in his mind, and then there was the whole W situation. *I hope he doesn't do anything nasty.*

Poor Tim was in for a surprise. Several surprises, actually. The first one came as he checked the alarm clock by his bed. Tim blinked in disbelief, and it took him a moment to process the information. "TWENTY PAST TEN?" he screamed, jumping out of bed as if struck by lightning, and leaping out of his pajamas. "I'm late. I'm late. I'm SUPER MEGA LATE!"

Why hadn't the alarm gone off? Why hadn't his mom woken him up before leaving for work? And why hadn't Oskar checked on him before heading to school? Those were all great questions, but he was in too much of a hurry to ask them, or brush his teeth, or wash his face, or even have some breakfast. He got dressed in record time, picked up his backpack, and raced downstairs like a spiky-haired maniac.

The next surprise came as Tim stormed into school and a terrible stench hit him. It smelled like someone had thrown a pot of sweaty-sock stew at his head. He gagged, pinching his nose. *What's with that smell?*

Tim scanned the lobby and noticed a group of students, also pinching *their* noses, gathered around the announcement wall. He frowned and moved closer to investigate.

"What a jerk!" said one of the kids.

"Who does he think he is?" said another.

"He's a monster!" said a third. "And a thief! What a waste of French cheese!"

French cheese? Thief? Who are they talking about? An uneasy feeling crept over Tim. *What if . . . NO.* He stopped himself. *Don't be silly. This has nothing to do with me. Everyone likes me now. I'm a star!* Tim tried to grin, but his smile didn't last. Because when he peeked through a gap in the crowd, he discovered the message that someone had written in big stinky cheesy letters on the wall:

I'M THE BEST AND YOU ALL ? STINK.
— TIM SULLIVAN

Tim let out a loud **GASP!** and twenty pairs of eyes fell upon him. He took a step back, shaking his head in panic while cold sweat dripped off his forehead. *I-i-it wasn't me! I—I—I didn't write that!* he wanted to say, but the words wouldn't come out. And even if they had, would it have made any difference? Judging from the way everyone was looking at him, Tim didn't think so. So he did what anyone else in his situation would've done.

Tim raced down the hallway, turned left at the corner, and almost crashed into a group of girls who were walking in his direction. Tim stopped, startled. One of the girls was Zoe, but he'd never seen her so upset. She walked with her eyes cast down, her face all puffy and red, almost as if she'd been crying.

"W-w-what happened?" Tim asked.

Zoe's eyes met his, and then the unthinkable happened. She burst into tears, hid her face in her hands, and ran off toward the playground!

"YOU AGAIN?" yelled one of Zoe's companions, frowning. "How dare you come back after what you've done?"

"You're the worst!" said another.

"Go away!" added the third.

Tim wanted—NO, needed—to understand what was going on. He hadn't done anything to upset Zoe. But clearly, this was not the right time to figure that out, because the three girls looked at him like starving lionesses about to pounce on their prey. He backed away with a sick feeling in the pit of his stomach. *Nothing makes any sense!* And just when it looked as if things couldn't get any weirder, a door burst open to his right, a pair of strong hands grabbed him by the arm, and he was pulled into complete darkness.

CHAPTER 19
THE IMPOSTOR

Tim didn't even get a chance to struggle.

"Who are you? What have you done with my best friend? And why are you trying to frame him? Answer me or you'll regret it!" his attacker yelled, shaking him like a rag doll.

Tim recognized the voice immediately. "TITO?" he screamed in surprise.

The shaking stopped and a light went on, revealing to Tim that he was inside a storage room and that it was indeed Tito who was holding him there.

Tim squirmed out of his friend's iron grasp. "Are you nuts?" he cried. "You almost turned my brain into scrambled eggs! What's wrong with you?"

Tito stared into Tim's eyes. "It's really you, thank goodness!" he said, squeezing him into a hug. "Sorry about that. I thought you were the other one. Where have you been?"

"I overslept," Tim said. But then, "Wait, what 'other one' are you talking about?" he asked, desperate to make sense of all the weird things that were happening.

"You know. Your evil twin," said Tito. "The one who's spent the morning making everyone hate you. He tried to fool me too, but I could tell he wasn't you. And then he ran away before I could stop him."

Tim frowned. An evil twin would explain a lot of what had happened that morning. There was just a tiny problem. HE DIDN'T HAVE AN EVIL TWIN!

Suddenly Ms. Crawley's voice boomed through the school's PA system:

Attention, please. Due to a terrible incident involving French cheese, all classes have been canceled. You may all go home EXCEPT TIM SULLIVAN. Tim, please report immediately to the principal's office.

"Ugh, this is a nightmare," said Tim, annoyed. "I guess I'd better go."

Tim reemerged into the corridor and saw something that made his jaw drop. It was him! Well, not *him* him but someone looking exactly like HIM. It was a fake, a pretender, AN IMPOSTOR!

"See? I told you!" said Tito, pointing at the look-alike. "You have an evil twin!"

What in the . . . ? Tim had no idea how or why this was happening. Evil twins don't pop out of nowhere. Unless . . . Where was Oskar? Did he have anything to do with it? The dinosaur was certainly smart enough to create an evil clone. But he wouldn't do such a thing, right? They were friends! Tim decided to focus on the problem at hand. Impostor-Tim was carrying a huge bottle of chocolate syrup and was headed straight toward Ms. Crawley's office. "We have to stop him!" cried Tim.

But by the time Tim and Tito reached the principal's office, evil-Tim was already gone. Tim peeked through the door and found Ms. Crawley sitting at her desk, frozen in shock, looking like a giant breadstick drenched in chocolate sauce.

"Tim, dear," the principal mumbled, keeping her usual nice tone. "Thanks for the dessert, but I think we have to talk."

Tim didn't have time to talk, though. He was being framed, and the only way to prove his innocence was to catch the impostor. Unfortunately, evil-Tim was nowhere to be seen.

"Darn it, we've lost him!" Tim said, stomping his foot in rage. "He's so fast!"

"He is, but it doesn't matter," said Tito, wiping something off the floor and then placing it in his mouth. Tim wrinkled his nose in disgust. "Yup, just what I thought," said Tito, laughing. "He's left a trail."

The two friends followed the chocolate drip marks out the fire exit, around the duck pond, and all the way to the edge of the school grounds. There the last traces of syrup disappeared into the janitor's toolshed.

"He's inside," whispered Tito with a grin. "We've got him!"

Tim grabbed the door handle, but it wouldn't budge—it was locked.

But not for long! Tito took a step back and . . . **BAM!** HE KICKED THE DOOR OPEN.

CHAPTER 20
REVENGE

The toolshed was dimly lit by a single light bulb hanging from the ceiling. It was a small room, with dusty shelves on the left, and mountains of boxes on the right. Gardening tools and cleaning supplies were everywhere, and right in the middle of it all stood Tim's evil twin.

"You're trapped!" said Tito, taking a step forward.

Tim stood back. Something about fake-Tim was giving him the creeps.

"Start talking!" continued Tito, raising his fist. "Why are you pretending to be Tim?"

Evil-Tim laughed, but his laughter sounded more like a creepy buzz.

"Be careful, Tito . . . ," whispered Tim, feeling goose bumps down his neck.

"Don't worry, I've got this," said Tito, advancing toward the impostor. "He's coming with us, and he's going to tell everyone the truth!"

But when Tito reached out to grab fake-Tim's arm, his hand went right through it!

Tito jumped back. "EW! ¿Qué es esto?" he asked, shaking off hundreds of insects that were now crawling on his hand.

"IT'S NOT HUMAN!" yelled Tim. "It looks like—It looks like . . ." Horror washed over him. "A SWARM OF BUGS!"

The shed echoed with evil laughter, but it wasn't coming from the creature's mouth. Tim flinched as a shadow emerged from behind a pile of boxes. "Oh, Shimmy Timmy, you're so perceptive," said a familiar voice. "I guess it's time for the big reveal."

Yup, it was W. And he was wearing Oskar's Bug Brain Booster 3.0.

Tim jolted in surprise. "That's impossible!" he said, rummaging through his backpack and confirming, to his dismay, that Oskar's device was missing. "W-w-what are you doing with that?"

W grinned. "Oh, did you really think that you could humiliate me, take my PopPop Pearls, and steal all the glory that I rightfully deserved—without facing any consequences?" he asked. "You used this device to cheat, so now it's only fair that I use it to destroy you."

Tim's face turned whiter than the inside of a ghost's wardrobe. His worst nightmare had come true, and he hadn't even worried about it this time! "I—I—I didn't mean to cheat," he stuttered. "I-I-I just got carried away. And anyway, I never wanted your PopPop Pearls in the first place!" Tim took the pack of candy from his pocket and extended it toward his nemesis. "Here, take it, but stop this. W, please!" he implored.

"Yes, you don't deserve that," said W, snatching the candy away. "But don't think that will be enough. I'm going to make sure that no one ever wants to talk to you again. And guess what? You only have yourself to blame."

Tim hesitated. W . . . had a point. This whole mess was his fault. *I should've known better than to use one of Oskar's devices to win!*

"Don't listen to him. He's taking it too far," said Tito. Then he glared at the bully, "Stop messing with my best friend immediately, or—"

W snapped his fingers, and the bugs in the room swarmed into a frenzy. "Or what?" he asked with a smug smile.

Fear seeped into Tim's bones, but Tito humphed and cracked his knuckles. "You think I'm scared of a few bugs?" he sneered, reaching out to one of the shelves and picking up a pair of flyswatters. "I'm going to squash your little friends silly, and once I'm done, you're going to tell everyone what you've been up to," he yelled, wielding the flyswatters like nunchakus. "We, the Delgados, are deadly with the matamoscas!"

Tito's unwavering confidence seemed to take W by surprise, but then he grinned. "We'll see about that," he said as he reached up to the helmet and cranked the intensity dial all the way up.

This could be troublesome!

PART 3

IT'S A BUG'S WORLD

It's a bug's world
after all. It's a bug's
world after all. . . .

CHAPTER 21

HERE WE GO AGAIN

The ground started shaking. "Don't do this!" Tim yelled. "Please!"

But W wasn't listening. He roared in laughter as more and more insects joined the swarm to create a monstrous creature that grew bigger, and bigger, and bigger.

Tim struggled to keep the worries out of his head, but reality was already set on a terrible course.

The creature turned around . . . and plucked the helmet off W's head!

"What are you doing?" W shrieked. "That's mine. Return it immediately!" he commanded, flailing his arms in the air in a futile attempt to recover the device. "It's an order!"

The creature's answer sent a chill down Tim's back. "We're done taking orders from humans," it buzzed. "It's time for us arthropods to show you who's boss." And with that, the monster opened its mouth and **CHOMP!**

And now that that's safely tucked away . . .

It swallowed the helmet whole.

Tim's mind flooded with equal parts fear and guilt. Barely any time had passed since Oskar's deranged AI had tried to destroy the world by getting rid of anything that was funny, good, or tasty. And now Tim had done it AGAIN! Humanity was in grave danger because of an overpowered maniac that he'd helped create. What would it be this time? What terrible thing was that creepy monster planning to do?

Tim didn't have to wait to find out. His thoughts were interrupted by a pretty self-explanatory song.

We've been squished, we've been squashed, we've been smushed, we've been smashed. We've been flicked, we've been trapped, we've been swatted, we've been zapped. We've been whacked with rackets, we've been hit with a shoe. Can you guess which of these we'll be doing to you?

As the creature sang the last verse of the song, it reached out and caught W in its massive hand.

"HEEEELP! HEEEELP!" the kid squealed in panic, his feet dangling in the air.

Faster than you could say "bug off," Tito burst into action and started whacking the creature's arm with his flyswatters.

SPLAT! SPLAT! SPLAT!

"Let him go, you filthy bicho!" he screamed. But for every bug Tito managed to smash, twenty more joined in, and within seconds, Tito was fighting not to get caught himself.

At the sight of his best friend's imminent danger, Tim snapped out of his stupor. The swarm had grown too big for the shed, and the entire structure was creaking under the mounting pressure. "We have to leave!" he yelled.

"But what about W?" Tito asked.

"NO! Don't leave me!" W cried. "PLEAAAASE!"

Tim groaned. Despite W's terrible meanness, he didn't deserve to suffer such a cruel fate. But was there anything Tim could do about it? Regardless of what Tito thought, Tim was no superhero. He was . . . a MESS! All he ever did was mess things up!

A mess . . . a mess . . . Wait a minute, that's it! Tim thought. A BIG mess could be what they needed right now. Tim scanned the room and found just the object he was looking for.

"RUUUUUUUUN!" Tim yelled as he unloaded the fire extinguisher onto the creepy creature, spraying foam left and right like a firefighter gone berserk. The swarm buzzed in anger while the room started to fill with a thick white mist. Tim couldn't see a thing. Did it work?

A second later a shadow broke through the foamy cloud. It was Tito, and he had W in tow. "¡Vámonos!" Tito screamed, motioning for Tim to follow.

Tim didn't need to be told twice. He let go of the fire extinguisher and broke into a run.

They were out, sprinting through the play-ground, when Tim looked back and noticed a dark cloud gathering above the toolshed. Tim's eyes widened. That thing wasn't a cloud.

They were reinforcements.

Suddenly a thundering buzz rattled the wooden structure, and an eerie tune rang in the air:

We've been squished, we've been squashed . . .

CHAPTER 22
OUT-HERO'ED

Tim and Tito stood behind one of the cafeteria's windows, their eyes glued to the freak show taking place right in front of them. The bug monster, now a towering giant twice as tall as the school building, was standing on the athletic field, giving a speech to hundreds of millions of bugs that buzzed, chirped, hummed, hissed, and cheered from the bleachers.

The creature had grown in more ways than size, though. It had also grown way more disgusting. It had eight floppy arms, a long hairy body, two pointy antennas, and to round it all out, a creepy humanlike head! The monster was straight out of a nightmare, and Tim was glad that Ms. Crawley had sent everyone home earlier that morning.

Tito leaned toward Tim's ear. "It's the Kraaaaken-pillaaaar!" he whispered in an ominous voice.

A tiny part of Tim's brain found Tito's joke funny. The rest didn't; it was too busy freaking out about the ginormous bug monster planning to take over the world!

"Rejoice, friends, for the Age of Arthropods starts today," said the Krakenpillar. (It was actually a good name!) "We're your new king. You may call us LORD SWARM. We bring you the gift of intelligence and speech, and command you to join us in this most glorious hour."

The insects in the stands buzzed, chirped, hummed, hissed, and cheered. The monster continued: "Find the humans and bring them all to us. We'll teach them their new place in this, OUR kingdom."

"Get down!" Tim yelled, throwing himself to the floor to avoid being spotted as the creepy critter assembly broke up and spread out in all directions. Tim landed next to W, who hadn't moved, or said a word—no apologies, no thank-yous, nothing!—since they'd rescued him. Was he still in shock? Or was W so stuck-up that he wasn't capable of gratitude? Tim wondered.

"We can't hide here like cowards," said Tito, refusing to move away from the window. "We have to go out there and stop that bugger before it's too late!"

Tito's defiance against unsurmountable odds was nowhere as surprising to Tim as W's reaction. "Haven't you seen the size of that thing?" the snooty kid snapped. "You can't do that! The moment you get out there, you're doomed. Tell him, Tim!"

Tim couldn't believe what he was hearing. Was W concerned for someone other than himself? That's what it looked like, right? Not only that but he'd also chosen to call him Tim instead of Shimmy Timmy. Was that his way of showing them some gratitude? Could he . . . have changed?

It was a confusing thought. That aside, W made a very good point; leaving the safety of the school was a *terrible* idea. And yet, there was no doubt in Tim's mind that that was exactly what he had to do. Why? Because there was one single being in the entire world who might be able to stop that madness: Oskar. What a terrible day for him to skip school!

"You should stay here and hide as best you can," Tim told W, sounding braver than he felt. "Don't worry, we've got this. Tito and I will go outside and look for help."

Tim could tell that W had expected a different reaction from him. The boy stared at Tim open-mouthed, his face twisted in an expression of complete puzzlement, as if he'd just found out that dogs say "MEOW" and lay purple eggs every second Thursday, or that the earth is shaped like a pepperoni pizza with a cheesy crust.

I know. I'm also surprised, thought Tim, who'd rather suffer through one of Oskar's three-hour-long comedy specials than leave the safety of the school.

But then a flicker of rage flashed through W's eyes. "Yeah, right, wouldn't you like that?" W lashed out, leaping off the floor. "Do you really think that I'll stand back while you swoop in and play the hero? You sneaky hedgehog. You want to steal my spotlight once again!"

Tim blinked twice. *What in the . . . ?*

"But let me tell you something, Shimmy Timmy," W continued. "You're no hero. You're less than a zit on a hero's mighty nose! I'm a HERO. And it is I, William Woodrow Wiggle the Third, who will stand up to that monster and save the day!"

And with those words, W exited the cafeteria.

"Should we . . . try to stop him?" Tito asked.

Tim shook his head and shrugged. That kid was a lost cause. And they had no time to waste.

CHAPTER 23
MISSION IMPOSSIBLE

The mission was clear. To save everyone, they had to find Oskar, tell him what was going on, and hope that somehow he could find a way to fix things. There was just a tiny problem. How were they going to make it all the way to Oskar's lair without getting caught?

It looked like an impossible mission. Even if they somehow managed to sneak by the Krakenpillar, they'd still have to deal with the millions of insects buzzing around the streets, looking for humans.

"It can't be done," sighed Tim. "We'd have to literally become invisible to be able to pull off something like that."

"Not necessarily," said Tito with a cryptic grin. "All we need, really, is to blend in."

"What do you mean?" asked Tim, puzzled.

Tito smiled. "Follow me!"

Tim followed his friend all the way to the visual-arts classroom, where Tito began raiding the arts and crafts closet. Ten minutes later he was done.

TA-DA!

"What do you think?" Tito asked while he added the final touches to the costumes that he'd built out of multicolored pipe cleaners, pom-poms, sheets of cardboard, and an awful lot of tape.

Tim had no words . . . or very few.

"Do you really expect us to be able to fool the bugs out there with these costumes?" he asked, hoping that his friend would realize how silly his plan was.

"Yes," Tito answered. "I'm one hundred percent positive."

Tim racked his brain, trying to find a better alternative, but eventually (and reluctantly) he gave in. *There's no other option,* he thought, and shrugged, trying not to dwell on all the things that could go wrong with what they were about to do. With any luck, they wouldn't meet any insects. That seemed to be their only chance.

Luck, however, wasn't on their side, because no sooner had they set foot on the street when they came across a grasshopper. Tim froze on the spot.

"Relax, it'll be fine," Tito whispered. "Follow my lead."

"Buzzup?" Tito said, nodding at the grass-hopper.

"Buzzup!" the grasshopper replied, bouncing away without giving them a second glance.

Tim was dumbfounded. He couldn't believe it. It had worked! *HOW?*

"You see, I told you," said Tito. "These costumes are the perfect camouflage."

Tim rolled his eyes. The costumes were so terrible that they wouldn't have fooled a blind earthworm. The key to Tito's success was something else altogether, and it could only be one thing: HIS CONFIDENCE!

Thankfully, unlike Tim, Tito had an almost infinite supply of self-confidence. And that's how six spiders, five bees, four beetles, three fleas, two mosquitoes, and one cockroach later, the two friends had made it all the way to Oskar's lair.

CHAPTER 24

BIG PROBLEM, TINY ROBOT

What Tim and Tito found when they stormed into Oskar's lair was weird even by Tim's time-traveling neighbor's standards. Oskar was lying on the floor, hugging a green pillow, fast asleep atop a smelly pool of pickle juice.

All around him were piles upon piles of empty pickle jars, which Tim recognized as the ones that W had delivered the day before.

But Tim had more urgent business than dwelling on his prehistoric friend's unhealthy lifestyle choices. "Oskar, WAKE UP. We have a HUGE problem!" he yelled.

"Five more minutes," the dinosaur grunted, shifting position. "I was working all night on a secret"—he yawned—"project."

Yeah, right. "Come on, I'm serious. This is urgent!" said Tim, losing his patience.

Oskar stretched his short arms, opened his eyes, blinked twice, and broke into laughter. **"WHY ARE YOU DRESSED LIKE THAT?"**

Tim tried to explain, but Oskar didn't stop laughing until they took off their costumes. "Okay, we're back to normal. Will you listen now?" Tim asked.

Oskar, still giggling, nodded, and so Tim was finally able to give him a rundown of the terrible events of that morning.

"Um, I thought this might happen," said Oskar after Tim had finished.

Tim and Tito looked at each other in shock.

"Oh yes," admitted the dinosaur. "Using the full power of the Bug Brain Booster 3.0 had a ninety-six-point-eight percent chance of ending up in an insect rebellion against humanity. That's why I gave it to you on the lowest setting."

"I see," said Tim, his blood starting to boil.

And didn't it occur to you that WE SHOULD'VE KNOWN FROM THE VERY BEGINNING?

Oskar remained as cool as a cucumber. "Don't fret, my hairy friends. I've learned from my past mistakes, and now every time I build a new gadget, I plan for any eventuality. Here, let me show you," he said, flicking a switch on the wall.

At once, the floor parted, revealing some sort of vending machine. "Let's see, which one is it?" the dinosaur muttered, scanning the rows of blinking buttons. "This one's for street-racing piranhas. This one's for zombie chinchillas. Here's one for the rise of the tickle monster. . . . Here! Insects trying to take over the world. This is the one!"

Oskar pressed the button, and **THUD!** something dropped onto the machine's pickup box.

Tim and Tito moved closer as their pre-historic friend reached into the box. Tim swallowed hard, his heart beating with trepidation. What sort of marvelous hyper-advanced piece of gadgetry had the dinosaur built in preparation for the insect apocalypse?

"Here it is," announced Oskar. "The solution to all our problems . . . THE MEGA BUG SQUASHER 5.0!"

But what Oskar revealed was nothing more than a toy. A cool robot toy, sure, with some sort of helicopter on one arm, and a tennis racket on the other, but a toy all the same!

"This is no time to play around," said Tim. "The Krakenpillar is the size of a building. We need a real weapon. And fast!"

Oskar laughed. "You seem to forget that size doesn't matter when you have one of these," he said, revealing his Molecular Ginormizer 5.0. "Let's go outside so I can show you the true might of the ultimate weapon of insectoid destruction."

MOLECULAR GINORMIZER 5.0

CHAPTER 25

OOPS

Following Oskar's instructions, Tim and Tito had placed the robotic toy figure in the middle of Tim's backyard and now stood at a safe distance, watching the scene unfold.

"THIFF IFF GOING TO BFEE EPFFIC!" said Tito, who was munching on a pickle he'd found on the way out of Oskar's lair.

Tim nodded. Maybe Oskar's plan wasn't so ridiculous after all. Tim had already seen what Oskar's enlargement laser could do, so if that little thing ended up becoming a giant robot . . . *Yes, this could work!* he thought.

And so, for the first time that day, Tim relaxed.

You see, Tim was exhausted. The day had been a disaster so far, and he'd been trying really hard to keep his worries at bay to avoid making it even worse. So the moment he felt that things were going to be okay, he gave himself a tiny break and let his guard down. It was an unfortunate mistake, because when Oskar pulled the trigger, a dangerous thought crossed Tim's mind. *WHAT IF something goes wrong?*

Just like that, the impossible turned into unlikely, the unlikely into plausible, the plausible into possible, yada, yada, yada. And as the laser beam was about to hit the robotic toy, a fly that had been buzzing around the garden got in the way.

ZAP!

Tim gasped.

FLY

ROBOT

There it was, big like an elephant, hungry
like a hippo, hairy like a bear—the ten-thousand-
pound fly!

Tim was about to start screaming like a starving
monkey outside an all-you-can-eat buffet when
Tito stopped him. "Make no noise and stay still,"
he whispered. "It can't see us if we don't move. I
read that somewhere."

Somewhere? Tito didn't sound very convincing, but Tim didn't feel like testing his friend's theory, so he held his breath and froze on the spot.

Well, at least we still have the robot, Tim thought, trying to stay positive in order to keep any further worries from popping into his head. But then a yucky, slimy, slithering tongue emerged from the fly's mouth, and **CHOMP!** the robot was totally, completely GONE.

But apparently, the robotic snack wasn't filling enough for the fly, and so the tongue got moving again. This time it headed STRAIGHT TOWARD TIM!

CHAPTER 26
DÉJÀ VU

Which brings us back to where we started, with Tim and Tito freaking out as the tongue of the ten-thousand-pound fly wriggled toward them, until . . .

SLURP! The fly started to lick Tim, like a loving puppy greeting its best friend.

Tim wiped his face and looked at the insect with new eyes. Could it be? It had to be! "Margot?" he asked. "Is that you?"

As if in response, the massive fly did a flip, rolled over, sat on the ground, and shook Tim's hand. Those were the tricks that Tim had tried to teach her! There was no doubt. It was her.

"I'm so glad it's you, Margot!" said Tim, hugging the huge insect's hairy leg.

At that same moment, Oskar, who'd been on the other side of Margot, reappeared.

"BUZZ, BUZZ, BUZZ, BUZZ, BUZZ, BUZZ, BUZZ?" the dinosaur asked, looking at the ginormous insect.

"BUZZ, BUZZ, BUZZ, BUZZ!" buzzed Margot.

"Really? That's very interesting," said Oskar, scratching his chin.

Tim's and Tito's eyes bulged out of their sockets.

YOU SPEAK
FLY?

"I do," said Oskar in a matter-of-fact way. "I learned it by listening to the flies we had in the Late Cretaceous. They were as big as pigs, and they would never shut up. But flies these days are too small for me to hear them. Well, at least until now."

"That's amazing!" said Tim.

"Not really. It's an easy language to learn," explained Oskar. "It only has a single word."

"So, what did you ask her?" asked Tito.

"I asked her if she's being controlled by the Bug Brain Booster 3.0, but she swears she isn't. She hears the commands, but somehow she's able to ignore them. It's quite odd."

"I think I know why," said Tito. "When Tim released Margot, he ordered her not to take orders from anyone ever again."

"It's true, I did!" said Tim, recalling his farewell words. "Good for you, Margot!"

Margot was about to lick Tim's face all over again, but she stopped mid-action and raised her head instead.

"Look! I think she's receiving a message from the Bug Brain Booster 3.0," explained Oskar.

Suddenly Margot started to buzz in panic.

"BUZZ, BUZZ, BUZZ, BUZZ, BUZZ! BUZZ, BUZZ, BUZZ, BUZZ, BUZZ!" she buzzed.

"What? No way! Seriously?" asked Oskar. "Hey, you two, does the name 'Lord Swarm' ring any bells?"

"That's the Krakenpillar!" yelled Tito. "What has that bugger done now?"

Oskar shared the news. "Margot says that he's captured a human kid and is about to do something awful to him."

Tim clenched his fists. If anything happened to that poor kid, he would never forgive himself. "We have to stop that monster!"

"Sure," said Oskar. "We just need to destroy the Bug Brain Booster 3.0 hidden inside its body. There's a tiny problem, though. It will take me a while to put together another Mega Bug Squasher 5.0."

"BUZZ, BUZZ, BUZZ, BUZZ, BUZZ!" repeated Margot insistently.

Tim reached out and patted the trumpet-shaped mouth of the fly with long, soothing strokes. "It's okay, Margot, I understand," he said. "We don't have time for that. We must go NOW!"

"But how?" asked Tito. "We've thrown away our costumes, and without them the Krakenpillar will see us coming a mile away!"

Tim looked at Margot, Margot looked at Tim, and a smile formed on the boy's lips. Even though they didn't speak the same language, Tim knew somehow that they'd just had the same idea. "Are you sure you want to do this?" Tim asked the fly.

"BUZZ, BUZZ, BUZZ, BUZZ, BUZZ," Margot answered.

Tim didn't need Oskar to translate. Her message was loud and clear: "That's what friends are for."

Meanwhile, live on TV . . .

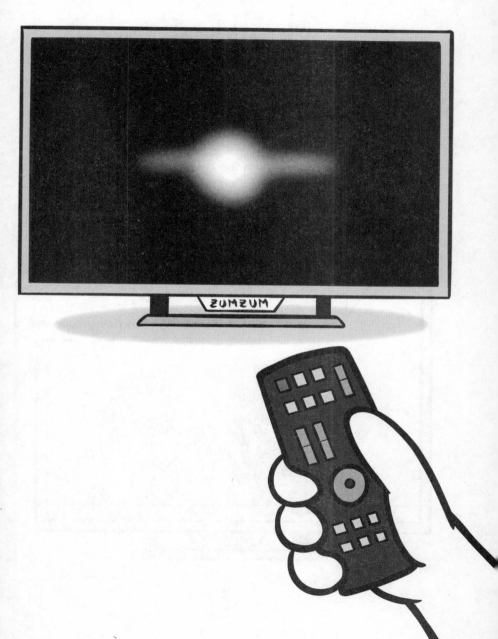

CHAPTER 27

M-BEE-C

Right, and talking about appetizing, I'd like to remind our audience that *Flick That Human!* is brought to you by Red Bug, the only sugar-free brain-boosting energy drink made by and for bugs.

Before we start, Giannina, could you explain to our new viewers how *Flick That Human!* works?

Certainly. It's simple. Our human contestant, who has been wrapped in a beautiful silk cocoon, will be flicked toward a target that's been drawn on a sticky trap. Points will be awarded for three categories: comedic performance, difficulty of the tricks performed while in the air, and landing accuracy.

Hi, Barry. That has proven to be a very controversial topic. A group of stud-ants told me that we should flick him using a gigantic thumb,

while a family of roaches assured me that a well-positioned flip-flop flick would prove to be a much more effective method. There's one thing everybug agrees on, though: We should flick that human REAL GOOD!

Indeed, we should. Thank you, Johnny.

We're connecting now to Flicker Stadium, where our supreme leader just arrived. And look at that! The crowd is going wilder than a stick bug on a traffic circle.

ZUMZUM

They need no introduction, but we'll introduce them anyway. Let's give a warm welcome to the creator of the new world, the magnificent, the un-smashed, the un-zappable, the very first of their name, king of all insects, czar of the centipedes, emperor of the arachnids, protector of the realm, lord regent of the arthropod kingdom, flicker of humans, and true and rightful master of the world, LOOOOORD SWAAAARM!

BRAVO! BRAVO! I'm so excited!

Now Lord Swarm will choose today's flicking tool. Will it be the giant flip-flop? Or perhaps the rolled newspaper?

And they choose . . . I can't believe it. It's the humongous flyswatter!

CHAPTER 28

A GIANT FLY TO THE RESCUE!

Tim screamed more in the next few minutes than in all of the previous nine years of his life combined. Riding Margot to save the day had seemed like a decent idea back when he'd been standing safely on the ground. But as he, Tito, and Oskar dove down from over one thousand feet of elevation toward a terrifying flyswatter-wielding monster, he secretly wished that he'd kept his mouth shut. He was no superhero, and this . . . THIS was his most terrible idea ever!

Could things get even worse?

"Guys, the Krakenpillar is aiming that flyswatter in our direction," said Tito. "What's the plan?"

Tito and Oskar turned toward Tim. Of course they did! He'd acted as if he'd hatched a plan, and they'd followed him without hesitation. Somehow they still trusted him even after all the times he'd messed things up. And yet, what was his plan, really? Had he seriously believed that they'd be able to swoop in riding the biggest fly ever imagined and rescue the prisoner right in front of the monster's eyes? That was ridiculous! *I have to tell them that I don't have a plan,* Tim realized. *But if I admit that to them, will they ever trust me again?*

Tim dreaded the answer, and the mere thought of it sent the butterflies in his stomach aflutter. *IF ONLY there were some other way. I know it's impossible, but wouldn't that be nice?*

Just like that, it happened. The impossible turned into unlikely, the unlikely into plausible, the plausible into possible, yada, yada, yada, and out of nowhere Margot sneezed, and guess what came flying out of her trunk?

It was THE MEGA BUG SQUASHER 5.0!

Quickly Oskar handed
Tim his enlargement
laser. . . .

Tim shot the toy in
midair, turning it into a
robotic giant of
insectoid doom. . . .

And Oskar jumped into the controlling pod
and prepared to face the Krakenpillar.

It had happened. Even if he didn't know how,
Tim had worried something helpful into reality.
And thanks to that, THERE WAS HOPE.

CHAPTER 29

THE GREAT BATTLE OF YUCK

The Krakenpillar swung the flyswatter toward the falling Mega Bug Squasher 5.0, but thanks to Oskar's quick reaction, the robot dodged with a flip, twisted two times in the air, and **HIYAH!** it karate-kicked the monster so hard that the Krakenpillar was sent flying across the athletic field.

The monster roared with fury, and within seconds the bug swarm had already changed shape and was back on the counterattack. **CLOMP, CLOMP, CLOMP.** The ground trembled as a black, six-legged creature charged toward Oskar. It had a long horn on its head, and its shell, hard and shiny, made it look less like an insect and more like an armored tank.

Fun fact! That's a rhinoceros beetle, also known as the Hercules beetle because of its strength. It can lift 850 times its own weight! (That's equivalent to a human lifting nine full-grown male elephants, by the way!)

The Mega Bug Squasher 5.0 stood its ground, and just as the beetle was about to skewer it, the robot jumped forward, did a somersault in mid-air, and landed on the creature's back. **SPLAT! SPLAT! SPLAT!** The blades on the robot's left arm pummeled the insectoid's body, sending thousands—if not millions—of bugs flying away in panic.

The beetle buzzed with rage and started shaking, and twisting, and thrashing, but the robot held on like a rodeo cowboy. But then **SWOOP!** the monster changed shape again under the robot's feet, and Oskar found himself trying to keep the Mega Bug Squasher 5.0 from falling off a rolling roly-poly.

Fun fact! Roly-polies, also called pill bugs, aren't actually bugs at all. They are terrestrial crustaceans, and they are related to shrimp. Did anyone order a roly-poly cocktail?

The robot wobbled clumsily as Oskar struggled to keep the giant machine balanced atop the creature. Then **SNAP!** the roly-poly unfurled its body and sent the Mega Bug Squasher 5.0 crashing to the ground.

The robot broke the fall with the thrusters on its back, but the monster was still on the attack, flying through the air like a cannonball.

With lightning-fast reflexes, Oskar drew the robot's right metallic arm back and swung its massive racket-shaped hand toward the incoming bug-ball.

But just as the roly-poly was about to get whacked, it morphed into a terrifying creature that caught the robot with its long, spiny legs and sliced through the racket with a deadly set of jaws.

Fun fact! That's a raspy cricket, the current record holder for the strongest jaws in the insect world. Even non-insects, like the mighty tarantula, are no match for this cricket!

CHAPTER 30
MEANWHILE

While Oskar battled the bug monster, Tim, Tito, and Margot took on a different yet equally important mission.

"Oskar doesn't need us. We should go help that kid," said Tim, pointing down toward a small wooden platform where the cocoon-wrapped contestant waited to be flicked. "The poor boy must be so scared."

No sooner had Margot landed than Tim jumped to the kid's rescue. Tim ripped through the silk strands that covered the boy's face and discovered, to his surprise, that the captured contestant was none other than W.

Tim hesitated. As you might recall, he and Tito had already rescued the snotty kid once earlier that day, and W's reaction afterward hadn't been all that pleasant.

"What should we do?" asked Tito, turning toward Tim. "He's always super-mean to you. Perhaps it's time to teach him a lesson."

W averted his eyes and remained silent. Tim frowned. What would happen if he saved W's life once again? Would W resent Tim even more after that? Would W lash out, and call Tim names, and make his life impossible for the rest of his days?

Perhaps. W was just that type of person. But it didn't matter. Tim sighed and continued to break apart the cocoon. *No one deserves to get hurt for my mistakes,* he thought. *No one, not even W.*

But as Tim removed the last thread tying the rich kid down, W broke into tears.

"I'M SORRY," the kid wailed. "I thought I was done for"—SOB—"and here you are, saving me again"—SOB, SOB—"despite how badly I've treated you."

Tim didn't know what to say, or how to react.

"Thank you, Tim," the spoiled kid continued, wiping his runny nose. "You're a good guy, you know?"—SOB—"And although I don't deserve your kindness or your forgiveness"—SOB, SOB, SOB—"would you like to try to be friends again?"

And so, for the second time in as many days, W extended his hand toward Tim. It was wet with snot and tears, and yet, this time around, Tim didn't hesitate.

It was a moving scene, but you might be wondering, *Okay, this is all very sweet, but what about Oskar? Wasn't he about to get chomped by a hungry cricket?*

Indeed he was, which was why the mood quickly shifted when a loud **GASP** escaped W's throat. "Your friend!" he screamed. "He's in trouble!"

CHAPTER 31
BRAVE

What Tim saw when he looked toward the battlefield shook him to his very core. *How is this possible? Oskar was supposed to win! I thought he didn't need us. And now . . .* With a knot in his stomach, Tim scanned the mountain of smoking rubble that used to be the Mega Bug Squasher 5.0. *Where is he?*

OSKAR

Tim found the *T. rex* lying on the grass. Next to him stood the Krakenpillar, who was taking powerful swings with his giant flyswatter. Tim gulped. The evil monster was warming up! Oskar was about to get whacked.

As usual, Tim was instantly overwhelmed with worries, guilt, and fear. *This is my fault! I shouldn't have left him on his own. Why didn't I keep an eye on him? What if . . .*

But while Tim stood frozen by his own insecurities, Tito charged ahead. "If you touch my friend, I'll crush you!" he yelled, running toward the towering creature with no weapon other than his fists.

Startled, Tim followed Tito with his eyes. Didn't Tito realize that he had no chance against the Krakenpillar? Wasn't he afraid?

He does realize. He must be afraid. So then why . . . ? All of a sudden Tim understood. Tito was brave because he faced the odds and his own fear and CHOSE to put himself in danger to protect his friends.

Tim's eyes burned with the fire of determination. He could also make that choice.

Tim's brain raced as he considered his options. He had to rescue his friend, but that wasn't enough. He had to stop the Krakenpillar FOR GOOD. And the key to doing that was to destroy the Bug Brain Booster 3.0 inside its body. But how? If Oskar's giant robot hadn't been strong enough, then what would be?

A hand fell onto Tim's shoulder. "Whatever you're planning to do, I'm in," said W. "That's the least I can do."

At those words, something clicked in Tim's brain. "In that case, could I ask you a favor?"

TIM'S BRAIN

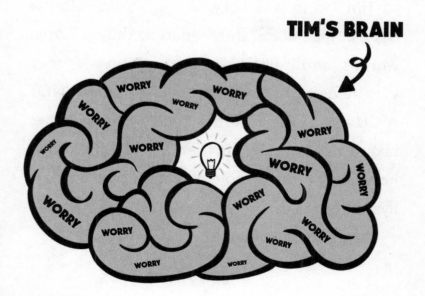

Tim's idea was risky. It was so ridiculously risky, in fact, that it threatened to drown Tim in worries, and it filled him to the brim with fear. Was he going to let that stop him, though? NOT A CHANCE! Because the choice was to either take a risk or have his friend, and who knows how many other people, flattened by a massive flyswatter.

It was an easy choice.

Tim and W jumped on Margot's back and stormed toward the Krakenpillar.

"Do you really think this will work?" W asked, his face stricken with worry.

"We're about to find out." Tim took a deep breath and removed the Molecular Ginormizer 5.0 from his pocket. *Okay, here goes nothing!* He tied one of Margot's hairs to his left leg. Then he stood up and yelled at the top of his lungs:

"HEY! LOOK HERE, YOU FURRY WORM!"

That got the Krakenpillar's attention. "WE'RE NOT A WORM!" it roared, twisting its body and raising the flyswatter for a deadly swing.

But Tim had other plans. And the instant the flyswatter started to rip through the air in his direction, Tim reached into his other pocket, took the pack of the poppiest PopPop Pearls in history that W had just agreed to return to him, threw it like a baseball, and pulled the laser trigger.

The pack of the poppiest PopPop Pearls in history flew toward the monster, growing, and growing, and growing, until **BAM!** it got SMASHED by the incoming flyswatter.

There was a bright flash of light and . . .

PART 4

CHAPTER 33

THE AFTERMATH

"He's here! I found him!"

"Tim, can you hear me? Are you okay? Please say something!"

Tim opened his eyes and stared at the three faces crowding around him. There was a boy, a *T. rex*, and a giant fly. If he hadn't felt as if a litter of cats had played a soccer match inside his head, he would've laughed. "Hey, guys, could you please stop spinning?"

It was a joke, but no one seemed to get it. They all looked so . . . concerned! It kind of made sense, though, Tim reasoned. He'd just been blasted off a speeding insect by the biggest candy explosion in history. So yeah, it was probably a bit too soon for humor.

"How long have I been out?" asked Tim.

"About fifteen minutes," explained Oskar. "We've been looking for you everywhere, and all this time you were here, hidden in this pile of salt."

"You're sooo lucky," said Tito. "If you hadn't landed here, you would've broken your head and half the bones in your body."

Oddly enough, Tim found that hilarious. Who knew that worrying up a salt-storm would end up being so useful? "So, did it work?" he asked, sitting up with a grunt. "Did we win?"

Tito smiled. "Yup. I don't know how you did it, but you blasted that bugger off the face of the planet. It looks like you saved the day once again, SUPER TIM!"

"Oh, I don't know who that is," said Tim, dusting the salt off his clothes. "I'm the Yucky Seasoner's best friend, in case you hadn't noticed." Everyone laughed at Tim's joke this time. "Anyway, it was a team effort. You, Oskar, Margot, and even—"

"Right, about Margot," Oskar interrupted. "I gotta take her somewhere safe, but she didn't want to leave without making sure you were okay."

"Leave? Why?" asked Tim, standing up.

"People are not too fond of insects right now," explained Tito. "And Margot is a whole lot of insect."

"Also, this place is swarming with journalists," added Oskar. "And if they see a giant fly, we could start a worldwide panic."

Tim sighed. He wasn't sure if he could handle another farewell, especially after everything he and Margot had lived through together. But he understood that it was what was best for her. *I've put her through so much already. She'll be happier far away from me,* he thought, reaching up to hug Margot's hairy head.

Almost as if she could read Tim's mind, the fly buzzed. "BUZZ, BUZZ, BUZZ, BUZZ, BUZZ!"

Oskar grinned. "She's asking me to tell you that this is not a goodbye. It's a 'Buzz you later,'" he translated.

The fly leaned down and placed a wet kiss on Tim's head. After that, Oskar climbed onto her back, and a moment later they were both gone.

"We should get going too," said Tito. "If my mom gets wind of what happened here, I'll need a crowbar to pry her off me. Do you think you can walk?"

Tim nodded but didn't move. "Wait! What about W?" he asked. "What happened to him? Is he okay?"

"Well . . . yes and no," Tito said, then hesitated. "It's complicated."

Tim frowned. "Complicated how?"

"I mean, he's fine," explained Tito. "He's back there talking with the journalists, but he's not–"

"Then what are we doing here?" said Tim, cutting his friend off and running in the direction Tito had pointed. "Let's go see him! Remember, W's a friend now."

"Hey!" Tim said, breaking through the crowd of journalists that surrounded his old nemesis. "I'm so relieved. . . ." He trailed off. Why was W giving him such an icy stare?

"Do I know you?" W asked, raising an eyebrow. "No, right? So why are you talking to me? Can't you see that I'm busy?"

Tim hesitated, confused. "B-b-but I . . ."

W humphed and turned his attention back to the journalists. "Seriously. If he wants to ask for my autograph, he should first learn some manners. Anyway, as I was saying: YES, it was me who single-handedly saved our city and, may I say, quite probably the world. I mean, I can't recall the details, but it's pretty obvious that I did, right? HOO, HOO, HOO, HOO!"

Tito took Tim's arm and pulled him away from the scene. Tim was so shocked that he didn't resist. "What's going on?" he asked finally.

"That's what I was trying to tell you before you stormed off," Tito said. "W also fell because of the explosion, and he hit his head pretty hard. It seems that all his memories from the last few days are . . . well, gone."

Tim gasped. *NO!*

"On top of that," Tito continued, "when the journalists found him lying on a pile of bugs, they assumed that he was the one who'd finished the swarm monster off. And as you've seen, he even believes that himself."

CHAPTER 34
PUCKLES

··· **WEDNESDAY** ···

"Wakey, wakey, sleepyhead!"

Oskar? thought Tim, slowly emerging from an unpleasant dream. *What time is it? Ugh. Who cares? School has been canceled today. And even if it hadn't been . . . I don't want to go. Everyone thinks that I'm a terrible person. And now that W can't remember a thing, there's no one to convince them otherwise!*

"Come on. I know you can hear me. Look, I brought you a surprise!"

"Go away!" Tim muttered, turning around and wrapping himself up like a bedsheet burrito. *I'm not in the mood. Life is so unfair.* He was about to fall asleep once again when he noticed an unfamiliar slurping sound. *Eh?* And the smell. *Ugh, is that vinegar?* And he also realized that his face was dripping wet.

Wait, is this . . . ? Is someone . . . ? LICKING MY FACE?

"Meet the pet of your dreams: Puckles, the world's first half-pug, half-pickle hybrid!" said Oskar. "I created him by combining the DNA of a pickle with the drool from Zoe's pug. What do you think? Isn't he awesome?"

"YOU DID WHAT?" asked Tim, so loudly that it startled Puckles, who was sitting on Tim's lap.

Tim stared at the strange creature cowering in front of him and couldn't help but feel a bit queasy. As far as pugs go, it was the ugliest pug ever. It was green, it was wrinkled, and its tail was a toothpick, for goodness' sake!

But then Puckles started whining, and Tim's apprehension melted away. Puckles was ugly, all right, but also kind of adorable. And those eyes, they were the puppiest puppy eyes he'd ever seen.

Despite his terrible mood, Tim couldn't help but smile, and when he did, Puckles leaped into his arms and licked his cheek.

"It tickles!" Tim laughed.

"I think he likes you," said Oskar.

"Thank you," said Tim. "You were right. Puckles is an awesome pet."

"An awesome pet for an awesome hero," Oskar added.

Tim's smile disappeared. Being a hero hadn't worked out too well for him. Margot was gone. W was back to being his mean old self and had stolen all his glory. Everyone in school thought that Tim was a selfish cheese-stealing jerk, and, worst of all, Zoe . . . Tim shuddered at the memory of Zoe's tears. He still didn't know what fake-Tim had told her, but the way she had reacted . . . *Zoe hates my guts.*

While Tim changed out of his pajamas, Puckles tried to cheer him up by prancing playfully around him while wagging his toothpick tail. It was a funny sight, but Tim didn't feel like laughing. "I need some air. I'm going for a walk," he said. Oskar remained where he was, but Puckles tried to follow Tim. "Alone," Tim added.

He dragged his feet down the stairs and walked toward the front door. No matter how hard he tried, things never seemed to work out for him.

But when he opened the door, there she was. ZOE.

CHAPTER 35

A NEW BEGINNING

Tim blinked twice to make sure he wasn't dreaming. "Z-Z-Zoe?" he asked.

"Oh, Tim, I'm so happy to see you!" she said with a big smile. "I've been worried sick. How are you feeling?"

Uh, shocked? Baffled? Confused? But instead he answered, "G-g-great, b-b-but aren't you mad at me?"

"Mad?" she asked, visibly surprised. "OH! You mean about what happened yesterday morning in school? Don't worry, Tito explained everything. I should've known that you'd never say such mean things to me."

Tim cheered inside. Tito was the best!

"And anyway," she continued, her cheeks turning pink, "how could I ever be mad at you? You saved us all!"

Tim blinked, unsure if he'd heard her right.

I–I–I did?

TIM'S REACTION ON THE OUTSIDE

TIM'S REACTION ON THE INSIDE

"Yeah. I know it's a secret, but you don't need to pretend with me," she whispered. "Everyone thinks that W saved the day, but I know it was you. I saw everything. I was crying out on the playground when that monster appeared, so I stayed hidden there the whole time."

Wait, WHAT? "Y-Y-YOU WERE THERE?"

"Yes, it was so scary," she continued. "All those bugs, and that enormous flyswatter . . . I was terrified. But then you showed up, and I couldn't believe it! And when the whole thing exploded, and I saw you falling . . ." Zoe shuddered. "I tried looking for you, but I couldn't find you. Anyway, I'm so happy to see that you're okay!"

Tim didn't know what to say. He stood still on the doorstep, too stunned to think.

"Oh, sorry," said Zoe. "You were going somewhere, right?"

I was . . . but I think I need to sit down after this, thought Tim.

"It's okay. I'll be going now. But I'll be seeing you

back in school, right?" Zoe paused a second and looked down at the floor. "And, Tim, seriously . . ."

Now it was Tim's turn to blush. Zoe's hug lasted little more than a second, but it marked the beginning of a new friendship and a new chapter in Tim's life. After Zoe left, Tim turned around and found Oskar grinning.

"So, are you ready for another adventure?" Oskar asked.

Tim smiled. He was. *This saving-the-world business might not be so bad after all. . . .*

ACKNOWLEDGMENTS

I'm forever grateful to my wife, best friend, and life partner, Jacko. I'm the luckiest man ever to be married to her. Thanks to my children, Andrea and Adrian, who are growing into amazing human beings despite my many flaws. Your love and kindness inspire me daily, and I couldn't be prouder of you two. Thanks also to my family and friends all over the world, and a special mention to my loving parents, Eni and Francisco.

Thanks to the team at the Bent Agency and in particular to my rock star agent, Gemma Cooper. You know when to push me and when to cheer me up, and you're always there when I need it. As if that wasn't enough, you're also super nice!

Thanks to my wonderful editors, Karen Nagel and Jessi Smith. I've told you this before, but I will say it again: you're a dream team! I'm already looking for a van to turn it into a "Pucklesmobile" and take you two around the country for a road trip/book tour. Thanks to Karin Paprocki for your guidance in bringing my characters to life; I feel I've become a better illustrator thanks to you. Thanks also to Bara MacNeill and Valerie Shea, with whom I communicate through comments on a Word file. Your attention to detail never ceases to amaze me, and whenever you spot one of my hidden Easter eggs, I can't help but smile. Finally, thanks to the rest of the Aladdin/Simon & Schuster team. Even though I don't get to work with you directly, I know that without each and every one of you this book wouldn't have been possible. You have my endless thanks!

I'd also like to thank my wonderful Mill Valley and Marin County neighbors for their kindness and support. I'm blessed to call this place home.

Finally, thanks to you, the reader. Thank you

for giving my wacky story a chance yet again. I hope you enjoyed reading this book as much as I enjoyed writing and illustrating it, and I hope you'll continue to join me, Tim, Tito, and Oskar in this wonderful journey. ¡Muchas gracias!

ABOUT THE AUTHOR

AXEL MAISY was born and raised in Barcelona and has lived most of his adult life in Hong Kong. He currently lives in Mill Valley, California, surrounded by magnificent redwood forests with lovely hiking trails that he wishes he'd visit more often. When he is not writing or drawing big-eyed characters, Axel spends his time watching squirrels and unsuccessfully chasing raccoons away from his vegetable garden.